Mama and Papa come to the door.
"It's getting late," says Mama. "Time for bed!"

"And please pick up your toys," says Papa.

The cubs are feeling sleepy.

"Oh, okay," they say.

"Now it's time to wash up," says Mama, leading them to the bathroom.

The cubs like to play with toy boats in the bath.

"I will read both books," says Papa.

"Yay!" say the cubs.

They climb into Papa's lap as he reads.

Curses!' cried Grizzlystiltskin as he flew into a fury and disappeared in a puff of smoke."

"No, read this one!"
say Sister and Honey.

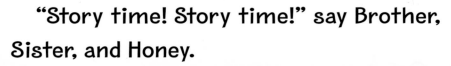

"Story time! Story time!" say Brother,
Sister, and Honey.
They get out their favorite bedtime books.
"Read this one!" says Brother.

"I know a clock rhyme," says Sister.
"Hickory, dickory, dock.
The mouse ran up the clock!"

And, of course, they like to blow bubbles—big, pink bubbles!

Mama looks at the clock in the hall.
"It's getting late!" she says.
"Time for your pajamas," says Papa.